OWN THE ZONE

OWN THE ZONE

ADAPTED BY MICHAEL ANTHONY STEELE

NEW YORK   TORONTO   LONDON   AUCKLAND   SYDNEY

MEXICO CITY   NEW DELHI   HONG KONG   BUENOS AIRES

ISBN 0-439-66319-9

Duel Masters, the Duel Masters logo, and characters' distinctive likenesses are trademarks of Wizards/Shogakukan/Mitsui-Kids. © 2004 Wizards/Shogakukan/Mitsui-Kids/ShoPro. Wizards of the Coast and its logo are trademarks of Wizards of the Coast, Inc.

HASBRO and its logo are trademarks of Hasbro and are used with permission. ©2004 HASBRO. All rights reserved.

Published by Scholastic Inc.
SCHOLASTIC and associated logos are trademarks and/or registered trademarks of Scholastic Inc.

12 11 10 9 8 7 6 5 4 3   4 5 6 7 8 9/0

Printed in the U.S.A.
First printing, September 2004

INTRODUCTION

The world as we know it isn't the world around us. There are awesome creatures living in five mysterious civilizations, realms of Nature, Fire, Water, Light, and Darkness. They can be brought into our world through an incredible card game — Duel Masters!

Though many kids and adults play this game, only the best can call forth these creatures. They are known as *Kaijudo Masters.*

This is the story of one junior duelist, or *Senpai*, unique among all others. His name is Shobu Kirafuda.

During the final match of the tournament, Shobu's luck seemed at an end. He had easily beaten all his previous opponents. However, the current champion, Joe Saiongi, blocked all of his attacks. He had even destroyed two of Shobu's shields. Shobu ran a hand through his spiky hair. He could see why this guy was the champ. Joe seemed to have the perfect deck for this battle and he knew how to use it.

Shobu glanced at the front row of the arena. As always, his friends were there to root for him —

Rekuta Kadoko and Sayuki Manaka. He could hear their cheers over the rest of the crowd.

Rekuta jumped to his feet, almost losing his glasses. "Go, Shobu!" he yelled.

"You can beat him!" Sayuki cheered, her hands tightly clasped together.

Shobu smiled and turned his attention back to the game.

"This is Gran Gure with 9000 power," Joe announced, as he drew a card from his deck. "It's capable of blocking any attack." He tossed the card onto the battle zone. "See how you like it, slinger."

"It's not over yet," Shobu said confidently.

Near the back row of the large arena, a man in dark sunglasses watched the match with great interest. "Let's see if Shori's son has the gift," he muttered to himself.

Back on the main floor, things seemed to be going worse for Shobu. He was now down to two shields. Shobu didn't seem nervous, though.

Joe reached for a card on the battle zone. "Say hello to Hanusa — Radiance Elemental!" Joe turned the card sideways, called *tapping*. When tapped, the card attacked one of Shobu's remaining shields. "*Ike!* Attack!"

Shobu simply smiled. "Oh, Joe?" He turned over the shield card.

"What?" Joe growled.

"I activate a shield trigger!" Shobu replied. "Tornado Flame!"

As Shobu placed the card onto the battle zone, a gust of wind blew Joe's card off the table. It was almost as if Shobu had summoned a *real* tornado.

"Ah, you're just wasting time, slinger," said Joe. "You'll be finished on my next turn!"

Joe attacked with two of his creatures, sending two of Shobu's cards to the graveyard. Shobu wasn't fazed. Instead, he raised his hand, ready to draw another card.

From the back of the arena, the man in dark sunglasses noticed something interesting — Shobu's hand glowed fiery red. The man was very surprised. Usually, only Kaijudo Masters could do something like that.

Shobu surprised everyone again when he whipped his glowing hand over his deck of cards. "Ya!" cried Shobu. The top card flew into the air, and then tumbled down to land in his open hand. Without looking, Shobu knew which card he'd drawn. "I summon Bolshack Dragon!"

"No!" yelled Joe.

"I can't believe it," Rekuta told Sayuki. "He may actually win the tournament!"

"This Bolshack Dragon is a double-breaker with a power of 6000-plus!" said Shobu. He placed the card into the battle zone. "And on top of that,

I'm going to use Burning Power to power up Nomad Hero Gigio." He placed a card onto another one. "This will not only destroy the rest of your shields, it will destroy the creature you were thinking of summoning!"

Sweat poured down Joe's face as he drew another card. "Shoot," he said in disgust. "This card won't do anything!"

"This is it!" yelled Rekuta. "This is the final play!"

"Come on, Shobu," Sayuki cheered. "You can do it!"

Joe selected another card from his hand and placed it into the battle zone. "This one is capable of blocking any attack," he said with a cackle.

"I summon the power of Scarlet Skyterror," Shobu said as he tapped one of the cards in the battle zone. "This will send all your blockers to the graveyard. *Ike!*"

"What?" Joe asked.

Shobu reached down and tapped the last card of the match. "Bolshack Dragon!" he yelled. "Finish it! *Todome da!*"

Joe beat the table with his fists. "Aaaaah!" he screamed.

"Shobu won the tournament!" shouted Sayuki. "He's the new champion!"

Rekuta thrust his fist in the air. "Own it! Own it! Own it!"

Outside the stadium, Shobu leapt as high as he could. He raised the golden trophy over his head. "I did it!" he yelled. "I'm Tournament Champion!"

"Congratulations!" said Sayuki.

"Man, I can't believe you won!" said Rekuta.

A red sports car pulled up alongside them. Behind the wheel was the man in the dark sunglasses. Shobu and his friends recognized him immediately.

"Is that Knight?" Sayuki asked.

"Yeah," Shobu replied with amazement. Knight was the world champion Kaijudo Master — the best.

Knight stepped out of the car and approached Shobu. His long, black coat rustled in the breeze. "That was a great game, Shobu," he said in a cool voice.

Shobu was a little surprised by the compliment. "Uh . . . thanks, Mr. Knight."

"Maybe you and I should duel sometime down at the Duel Center," said Knight. "You know, just for fun."

Shobu's jaw dropped. "You and me?" he asked. "That's a good one!"

Knight gave Shobu a sly smile. "Well, if you don't think you're good enough to take me on, that's okay. I understand if you're scared." He walked back to his car. "Very few people have the talent to challenge me."

Shobu was boiling inside. Champion or no champion, no one called him scared! "Okay, *Mr. Cool Sunglasses*," he said. "You've got yourself a match!"

Knight stopped and turned around. "I don't want just a match. I want your best."

"I always do my best," Shobu said proudly. "Besides, I never turn down a challenge."

"True," admitted Knight, "but you've never had a real duel."

"What are you saying?" Shobu demanded. "All the matches I've had aren't real?"

"That's not what I meant," replied Knight. "But there's a difference between playing in the schoolyard and real dueling." He reached into his pocket and pulled out a silver card case. "You're good kid, but you could be better." Knight removed a card from the case and slowly twirled it in his hand. "There are only a few of them in the world, but I

think you have what it takes to be a Kaijudo Master."

"Wow!" Rekuta cried. "So, you're looking for an apprentice and you think that Shobu could be the one?"

Knight smiled. "That's right."

Shobu looked at the trophy in his hand. "I've always wanted to be a real Kaijudo Master, and follow in the footsteps of my father." He looked back at Knight. "Do you really think I have what it takes? Because if you do, I'm more than ready to duel with you!"

"Oh, he's definitely ready, Mr. Knight," Sayuki declared.

Knight got back in his car. "Why don't you come by the Duel Center tomorrow afternoon and we'll see how good you really are?"

Shobu and his friends were speechless as they watched Knight drive away.

The next day, Shobu, Rekuta, and Sayuki entered the Duel Center and quickly found Knight's office. Inside, Knight had his back to them as he stared out a large window. A big trophy case lined one wall and a dueling table stood in the center of the room.

"Glad you could make it," Knight said as he turned to face them.

"I'm ready to duel," Shobu announced.

"I don't believe it!" Rekuta shouted. He pushed past Shobu and Sayuki to get to the trophy case. With his mouth open, he gazed at all the colorful trophies and medals. "That's the Intercontinental Championship Trophy from 1996, in Stockholm, Sweden!" He pointed to a glittering award. "And look! This is the National Trophy from Belize!" Rekuta pointed to a medal resting in a silk case. "And this one!" Rekuta said. "I have no idea what this is, but man, it looks really cool!"

"You must be the best duelist in the world!" exclaimed Sayuki.

"Well, that's what that medal says," Knight replied with a chuckle. He then turned his attention to Shobu. "But that's not why we're here. Are you ready?"

Shobu whipped out his deck. "Yeah, I got my cards right here! I'm going to own the zone!"

Rekuta and Sayuki sat on a bench beside the dueling table. Shobu stood at one end of the table while Knight stood across from him. Knight opened his silver card case and something very strange happened — as he reached for his cards, his hand began to glow red!

"That's a little different," Rekuta remarked.

"Oh, I don't like this," said Sayuki.

"Um . . . you're not going to psych me out," said Shobu. "I was taught by the best."

Knight's hand faded back to normal as he placed his deck onto the table. He slid the deck over to Shobu. Shobu slid Knight his deck, too, and they shuffled each other's cards. When they finished, they exchanged decks once more and began to put down their shield cards.

"I hear you're really good at swift attacks," said Knight. "You ready? *Ikuzo!*"

"*Koi!* Bring it on!" Shobu replied. "Now you're going to see my real game. I'm not going to hold anything back!"

Shobu drew Bronze-Arm Tribe card and

placed it into the battle zone. "What do you think of that move, Mr. Knight?"

"Interesting," Knight replied. "But if that's your best move, we've got a long way to go. Let me show you what a real Kaijudo Master would do." His hand hovered over one of the mana cards turned upside down behind his shields. Once again, his hand glowed red.

"What are you doing?" Shobu asked.

"You have to concentrate," Knight instructed. "In concentrating, mana is generated." A glowing, red sphere slowly rose from the mana card. Knight pulled a card from the top of his deck and held it up.

"Mana, give your power to this card."

Knight's hand glowed brighter as the red sphere flew toward it. It hit the card, disappearing inside it. The card itself began to glow.

"I summon Deadly Fighter Braid Claw!" Knight announced. He flung the card into the battle zone.

The creature pictured on the card seemed alive. In fact, Shobu swore he heard a hiss escape its deadly beak.

"Ah!" Shobu cried.

"Now," said Knight, "we can begin the *real* duel!"

Shobu didn't know what to think. The creature on the card was moving! Out of all the matches he'd played, nothing like this had ever happened.

"Remember," Knight reminded Shobu. "Concentrate before your next move."

Shobu held his hand over one of his mana cards and closed his eyes. "Okay, mana is generated." Nothing happened. Shobu drew a card from his deck and placed it onto the battle zone. "Okay, Knight. I summon Fatal Attacker Horvath." He smiled. "How was that?"

Knight sighed. "It's a good move, but not good enough." He held his hand over two mana cards. "Don't try to beat me, try to win." His hand glowed once more. "Now I summon Crimson Hammer!" Two more red orbs rose from the cards and entered Knight's Crimson Hammer card.

"That will destroy my Fatal Attacker Horvath!" cried Shobu.

Knight tapped another card on the battle zone. "Now I will attack your shields with Braid Claw. *Ike!*" A red beam of light flashed from Knight's card and hit one of Shobu's shield cards. The boy's card flew off the table.

Shobu jumped back. "Whoa!"

"Shobu's usually good at swift attacks," said Rekuta.

Sayuki covered her eyes. "I don't think I want to watch this."

"Swift attacks work in tournaments, Shobu,"

said Knight, "but they don't always work in life. If you're going to be a true Kaijudo Master — if you're going to understand your power — you can't just play from your head." Knight placed his hand on his chest. "You have to play from your heart. Remember, you don't have to beat me to win."

He keeps saying that, Shobu thought, *but what does it mean?*

It didn't matter. Shobu had never lost a match and he wasn't going to lose this one — even if it was against the world champion. He drew another card. "I'll beat you *and* win!" Shobu shouted.

"We shall see." replied Knight.

Shobu played as hard as he could. He ran through every strategy he knew and every play that had worked for him in the past.

Knight easily blocked all his moves. He destroyed his creature cards, and blew away his shields. Worst of all, it seemed that the harder

Shobu tried to beat Knight, the worse he was beaten.

"He only has one shield left," Rekuta reported. "He's going to lose!"

"No!" cried Sayuki.

Shobu dropped to his knees. He didn't know what to do. He couldn't concentrate. All he could think about was how he was going to lose.

"Sorry, kid," said Knight. "I thought you had the gift, but sometimes you just can't tell." He crossed his arms. "So . . . do you want to finish the duel, or do you just want to leave?"

I don't believe this, Shobu thought. *I only have one shield left. I don't have enough cards. I don't have the right cards. I can't possibly win.*

"It's okay, Shobu," Sayuki said, trying to console her friend. "You played a good one."

"Yeah," Rekuta agreed. "You really owned the zone."

Shobu hung his head. "I didn't own anything."

"Now you're starting to sound like a Kaijudo Master," said Knight.

Shobu shot Knight a sharp glance. "What?"

"Sounding like a Kaijudo Master and being one are still two different things," Knight replied. "If you continue to play me, I'm probably going to beat you. But I can beat you and you can still win. That's what owning the zone is all about." Knight picked up his deck. "But if you can't understand this concept, then you can't be a Kaijudo Master and you should quit."

"Okay." Shobu sighed. "I quit."

5

A much younger Shobu sat on his father's knee as he played with his dad's Duel Master cards. He enjoyed playing with the pretty cards. They had cool pictures on them, too.

"You like playing with my cards, don't you, Shobu?" his father asked.

"Yes," little Shobu replied. "It's fun."

"But sometimes you may be beaten," his father warned.

Shobu put the cards down. "Then I don't want to play."

Shobu's father picked up the dropped cards. "Oh, but you should play," he said. "It's important that you do your best. Then you will always win."

"Okay, Dad," Shobu said with a smile. He took the cards from his father.

"Promise?" his father asked.

"I promise," agreed Shobu.

"Trust in yourself," his father added, "and never give up."

Kneeling in Knight's office, Shobu remembered what his father had once told him. He wished he could talk to his father right now. He missed him very much.

Shobu stood. "I just remembered a promise I made to someone a long time ago." He clenched his fists. "I'm not going to quit. If I do my best and never give up, I'll always win." He picked up his cards from the table. "Okay, Mr. Knight, let's finish this!"

"I respect your decision," said Knight. "But

how are you going to fight back? You have only one shield left."

"It doesn't matter," Shobu replied. "A duel is like life — you never know what's going to happen."

Shobu's hand began to glow red as he passed it over his deck. The top card flew off the deck and into the air. It floated down and landed in his out-stretched hand.

Knight smiled. "That's it."

"I summon Bolshack Dragon," Shobu said, as he held his other hand over his mana cards. Six orbs rose from the cards and flew into the Bolshack Dragon card, making it glow. "If I do my best, I'll always win!"

"I want your best," said Knight.

Shobu placed the card into the battle zone. As he did so, he could almost feel the mighty dragon standing behind him.

"That's owning the zone," Knight said as he

drew a card.

Shobu played a great game against Knight. He destroyed two of Knight's shields and Bolshack Dragon even beat Knight's Scarlet Skyterror card. Shobu actually had a chance to win the duel!

"I summon Laa, Purification Enforcer," said Knight. He placed another glowing card into the battle zone. "Okay, Shobu, it's your move. Own the zone."

"*Hai!*" Shobu yelled. "Bolshack Dragon, attack shields now. *Ike!*"

"All right!" yelled Rekuta.

"Go, Shobu," cheered Sayuki.

"My turn," announced Knight. He tapped a single card in the battle zone, Holy Awe, which tapped all of Shobu's creatures. This was the beginning of the end for Shobu. Knight destroyed all of Shobu's creatures, leaving him helpless. During the next turn, Knight easily broke Shobu's remaining shields and then made his final attack.

"*Todome da!*"

The game was over and Knight had won.

"I can't believe it," said Shobu. "I lost."

"You played a good game, Shobu," said Knight. "But more importantly, you owned the zone."

6

Later that evening, Knight walked into the Master's office. Dressed in a black robe, the Master sat behind his desk. A dark hood concealed most of his face. Only a crooked smile and a long strand of gray hair gave away any of the man's true appearance.

"Does he have the gift?" the Master asked.

"He has potential," Knight replied.

"I want to know *exactly* how good Kirafuda's son is," the Master growled.

"I don't think he's ready," said Knight.

The Master brought his fist down upon his desk. "That is for *me* to decide!"

7

The next day at school, all Shobu could think about was what Knight had told him — that he had what it takes to become a Kaijudo Master. Could that be true? Shobu wanted to be a true Kaijudo Master like his father, but part of him was scared. Part of him knew that being a Kaijudo Master was more than just playing a game — much more. He wished he could ask his father for advice.

Shobu was so distracted, he dropped his deck of cards as he left his last class. "Oh, no!" He scrambled to pick them up. "They're going to get dust on them!"

Other students stepped around him as he crawled along the hallway. When Shobu reached for the last card, another hand grabbed it first. He looked up to see a girl with long, black hair holding it.

"Wow, this is cute," said the girl. "What is it?"

Shobu got to his feet. "That's one of my Duel Masters cards, and uh . . . you're bending it."

"Oh, sorry," the girl said as she handed it back. "What's a Drool Master?"

"'Drool Master?'" asked Rekuta as he exited the classroom.

Sayuki was right behind him. "It's called *Duel Masters!*"

"Oh, sorry again," said the girl. "That's a strange name for a bubble gum card."

"Actually, it's a strategy game," Sayuki explained.

The girl's face lit up. "Oh, I love strategy games. Is it like Go Fish?"

Shobu rolled his eyes. "Not really."

"I'm Mimi," said the girl. "Will you teach me how to play Drool . . . I mean Duel Masters?"

Now Shobu's face lit up. He never passed up a chance to duel. "Sure," he said. "Let's go own the zone!"

At the park, Mimi, Rekuta, and Sayuki watched as Shobu shuffled his cards atop the dueling table. Rekuta had attached a camera to his laptop so he could record Shobu's new moves.

"All right," said Shobu, "here's how it goes. When you start a duel, all you need are forty cards. There are hundreds of them to choose from and you can pick any forty you want."

After shuffling, Shobu placed five cards, facedown, on the table. "You put five shield cards down, then place a mana card upside down." Shobu put a

card behind his shields. "If you want to use it, you tap it." He turned the card sideways.

"But you didn't tap it, you turned it," said Mimi. "Why don't they just call it *turned*?"

Shobu sighed. "They just don't."

"Well, that seems silly," Mimi said huffily.

"Look, do you want to learn how to play?" asked Shobu.

Mimi put her head down. "Yes."

"Maybe she'll be able to understand better if you actually show her what a duel looks like," Rekuta suggested.

"Hey, two-tone head," a voice said behind them.

Shobu and his friends turned to see a thin boy with spiky red hair.

"My name is Jamira," said the boy. "Why don't you duel with me?"

"Sorry, we're all booked up this afternoon,"

said Sayuki. She pointed to Mimi. "This is an instructional match for our duel-ly challenged friend here."

"Then it doesn't matter who you duel." Jamira cracked his knuckles. "Besides, who better to give instructions than a master like me?" He stepped up to the dueling table.

Shobu never walked away from a challenge, even from a world champion like Knight. Yet somehow, this guy gave him the same feeling Knight first gave him. Who was he really? And why did he just show up wanting to duel?

Shobu gathered his cards. "I hope you play better than you look, Jamira," he said.

Back at the Duel Center, a hooded figure walked into the Master's office. "It's been reported that Jamira is now with Shobu," the figure said.

"Excellent," replied the Master. "Jamira will use any dirty trick in the book to win a duel." He smiled under his dark hood. "This is a great opportunity for us to see how capable Kirafuda's son is."

8

Shobu's friends watched as the two duelists shuffled each other's cards. Rekuta leaned forward to make sure Jamira wasn't cheating. Mimi held his laptop.

When they returned each other's decks, Jamira looked up at the sky. "Looks like rain. I hope you're not thinking of using it as an excuse to quit."

Everyone looked up at the approaching dark clouds. Shobu faced Jamira. "No way!" He laid out his cards. "*Ikuzo!* My shields are set."

"*Koi!*" Jamira replied. "Bring it on! Shields up!"

Rekuta nudged Mimi and pointed to the table. "Duelists first place five cards in front of each of them. They're called shields."

"That part I got," Mimi replied.

"Whoever breaks all of the opponent's shields and then makes a direct attack on the opponent will win," Rekuta explained. "That's a duel!"

Jamira crossed his arms. "I heard you're good at swift attacks, Shobu. So I'll be big about it, and let you go first."

"You're going to regret that later," Shobu replied. He placed a card in his mana section, then held his hand over it. His hand began to glow.

"Only creature cards are capable of attacking your opponent," Rekuta continued. "But you must have enough mana to summon a creature to attack."

Shobu concentrated until a small, red sphere rose from his mana card.

"Ooh, pretty," said Mimi.

"Let's try fire mana," said Shobu. "I summon Deadly Fighter Braid Claw!" The tiny, red orb flew into the card Shobu drew from his deck.

"Wowie-kazowie!" Mimi exclaimed.

"And that, Mimi," said Rekuta, "is what we call *summoning a creature*."

"Now I will make water mana," Jamira announced. A tiny, blue orb rose from his mana card. "I summon Marine Flower with this mana." The tiny sphere zipped into the Marine Flower card.

Whoa! Shobu thought. *Is Jamira a Kaijudo Master like Knight?*

"It's a blocker," Rekuta told Mimi. "It's capable of blocking attacks from your opponent!"

Shobu and Jamira played a fierce match. Shobu broke two of Jamira's shields, but lost three of his own. The entire duel played the same way. The harder Shobu tried, Jamira would still end up a little bit ahead.

"Hey!" Rekuta got to his feet and pointed to Jamira. "Every card he draws is something he can use for an attack!" he shouted. "If he wants a certain card, it just somehow appears!"

Shobu shrugged his shoulders. "I do the same thing, Rekuta."

"Yeah, but you're the hero," Rekuta replied.

"Stop with the ridiculous accusations!" Jamira roared. He pointed to Shobu. "Remember, he shuffled my deck before the match!"

"That's not true," said Mimi. "Shobu didn't shuffle your deck."

"What?" everyone asked.

"Remember?" asked Mimi. "Everybody looked up at the sky right after Shobu shuffled his deck." She pointed to Jamira. "I saw him switch decks."

"What?" Shobu, Rekuta, and Sayuki all asked in unison.

"Why didn't you tell us sooner?" asked Rekuta.

"I thought that's how you played," Mimi replied. Everyone stared at her. "Well, what do you want from me?" she asked. "I'm new at this."

Jamira laughed. "Poor little Shobu. You have

no proof."

"Well," said Mimi, "except that I've been recording the whole match with Rekuta's laptop."

Jamira's eyes widened. "Huh?"

"All right!" Rekuta cheered, as he leaned in to take a look.

Mimi played back the video of Shobu and Jamira getting ready for the match. Sure enough, when Shobu and the others looked at the dark clouds, Jamira reached into his pocket. He was about to pull something out when another figure entered the frame, blocking their view of Jamira.

"Hey, what's that?" Rekuta asked nervously. The person blocking the camera wore the same color shirt he did.

"It's your big, fat butt, that's what it is!" Sayuki yelled.

Mimi smiled at Shobu. "Never mind."

Jamira laughed and drew a card. "Okay,

Kirafuda, you're going down."

"You have no idea about the world of hurt you're going to be in," Shobu warned.

Jamira smirked as he tapped one of his creature cards. It destroyed one of Shobu's last two shields. "Oh, yeah?"

"Thanks, Jamira," Shobu said with a chuckle. "I was hoping you'd do that." He picked up the shield card and turned it over. "Now I'm going to activate my shield trigger. I cast Tornado Flame. *Ike!*" A whirlwind swept across the table and blew away Jamira's attacking card.

"Good. It's a shield trigger," said Rekuta.

"A what?" asked Mimi.

"If a broken shield was a shield trigger," Sayuki explained, "you can use the card right away!"

"Please, Shobu," said Jamira. "That move rarely works."

Shobu drew another card. "Then I summon

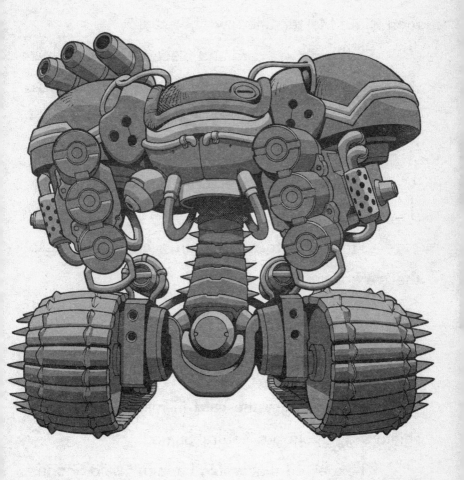

Rothus the Traveler."

Jamira chose a card and powered it with mana. "I'm still ahead of the game," he said. "I summon Night Master, Shadow of Decay!"

Shobu drew a card and placed it onto Rothus the Traveler. "And I cast Magma Gazer." Both cards glowed brightly.

"Whoa," said Mimi. "What just happened?"

Rekuta leaned closer. "He used a spell card to power up Rothus."

"I'm going to go out on a limb and guess that's a good thing," said Mimi.

Shobu tapped both cards. "Rothus, Attack! *Ike!*" A red beam shot across the table and hit one of Jamira's shields. The card flew off the table.

Jamira caught the card in midair. "You hit a shield trigger, Shobu. Natural Snare."

"I expected that would happen," said Shobu.

"What?" asked Jamira.

"When Natural Snare destroys a player's creature, it increases that player's mana," Shobu explained. "That will allow me to use my trump card. Thanks!"

Jamira grumbled as Shobu held out a glowing red hand. He whipped it over the deck and the top card flew into the air. It tumbled down to land in Shobu's waiting fingers. "I summon Bolshack Dragon!"

"Why did you wait and save Bolshack Dragon until now?" asked Jamira. "You've been in trouble all along!"

"Because, if you were using dirty tactics," Shobu replied, "I was sure that you would have a shield trigger hidden somewhere."

"I'm not out of it yet," Jamira growled.

"Oh yes, you are," Shobu announced. He tapped another card on the battle zone. "I attack with Scarlet Skyterror and send all of your blockers

to the graveyard!" A red beam shot from Skyterror, blasting Jamira's blockers off the table.

"My cards!" Jamira yelled, grasping at the air.

Shobu tapped Bolshack Dragon. "Double-break his shields! *Ike!*" Another beam shot across the table and blew away the last of Jamira's shield cards.

"Awesome!" Rekuta cried. "Now Jamira is not going to be able to attack Shobu in the next turn!"

Jamira looked at the cards in his hand. "Shoot! All out of creatures."

"All right, final blow," Shobu announced. "Bolshack Dragon, *Todome da!*"

For a split second, Shobu could actually see Bolshack Dragon as he attacked. His mouth blew a fiery plume toward his opponent. Jamira's eyes widened as the flames hit him square in the chest, knocking him to the ground.

"Oh yeah!" Shobu yelled. "Own the zone!"

Rekuta and Sayuki cheered.

"Did Shobu win?" Mimi asked.

Sayuki rolled her eyes. "Yes, Mimi, he won."

Jamira quickly gathered his cards and ran up the steps toward the street.

"Yeah, you better run!" Sayuki called after him.

Once at the top of the hill, Jamira turned and glared at Shobu. "I may have lost today," he yelled, "but one of the members from the Temple will defeat you for sure!"

As Jamira ran away, thunder boomed in the distance. A few drops of rain fell from the sky.

The Temple, huh? Shobu thought. *Why would someone from the Temple want to defeat me?*

Either way, it didn't matter. In the end, he had kept the promise to his father. Whether he won or lost, he had played his best. He also performed the way Knight had taught him. Shobu truly owned the zone.

He was well on his way to becoming a true Kaijudo Master!

10

Once again, the robed figure entered the Master's office. The Master himself sat facing the window, his back to his guest. He watched the rain beat against the glass.

"Master," said the figure. "Jamira has lost."

Underneath his black hood, a smile spread across the Master's face. "Excellent," he said. He allowed himself a small laugh.

The Master had big plans for Shobu Kirafuda.

Fuel the Duel

Get the **Duel Masters**™
2 Player Starter Set, packed
with everything you need
to start playing right away!

DuelMasters™
TRADING CARD GAME

Wizards
OF THE COAST
™